THEODORE

The Sloth Who Wants to RACE

To Marleigh, Max and Melody, editors extraordinaire.

Published by Penelope Pipp Publishing

www.penelopepipp.com

ISBN: 978-09882369-8-1 (Hardcover)
ISBN: 978-0-9882369-7-4 (Pbk)
Library of Congress Control Number: 2024918120

THEODORE
The Sloth Who Wants to RACE

Dr. Sam & J.L. McCreedy

Penelope Pipp Publishing

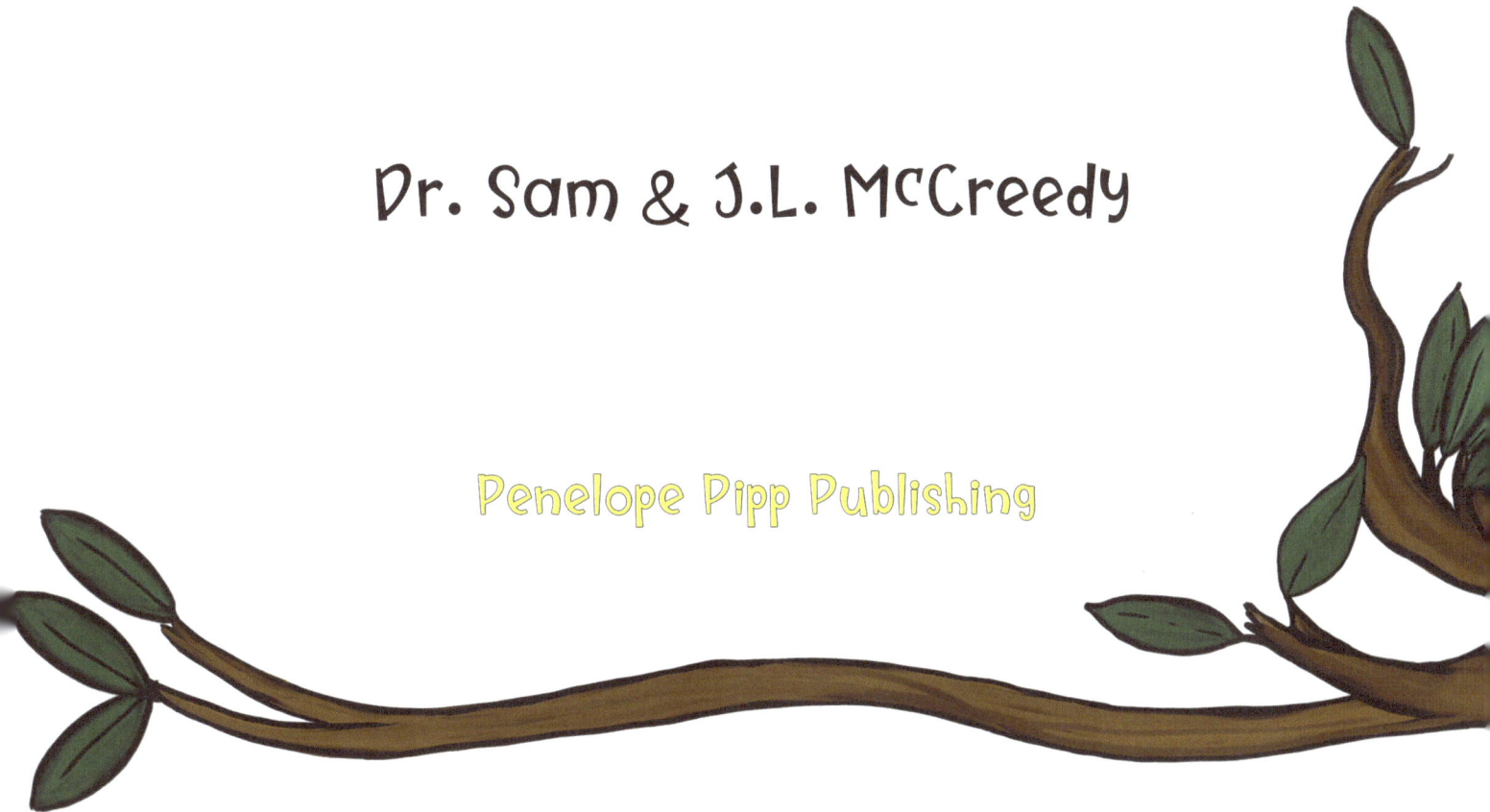

Chateau
Theo

Theodore lived in a tree
as sloths are apt to do.
Some sloths have toes
that number THREE
but Theo's numbered ...

TWO!

Most folks know that sloths are SLOW
and though this could have hurt him,
Theo never read that fact.
Of this, you can be certain.

EVERYTHING YOU
NEED TO KNOW!

"This book changed
my life!"
-Ophelia Folivora

THE BOOK OF SLOTH

THE BOOK
OF
SLOTH

I.M. Chillin

SLOTHS
'R'
SLOW

For Theo thought
he was quite quick
as 'tween
the vines
he'd creep.

(That is, after his usual thirteen hours of sleep.)

While he crawled, his forest friends
would gaze with looks of wonder,
and contemplate what sort of spell
that two-toed sloth was under.

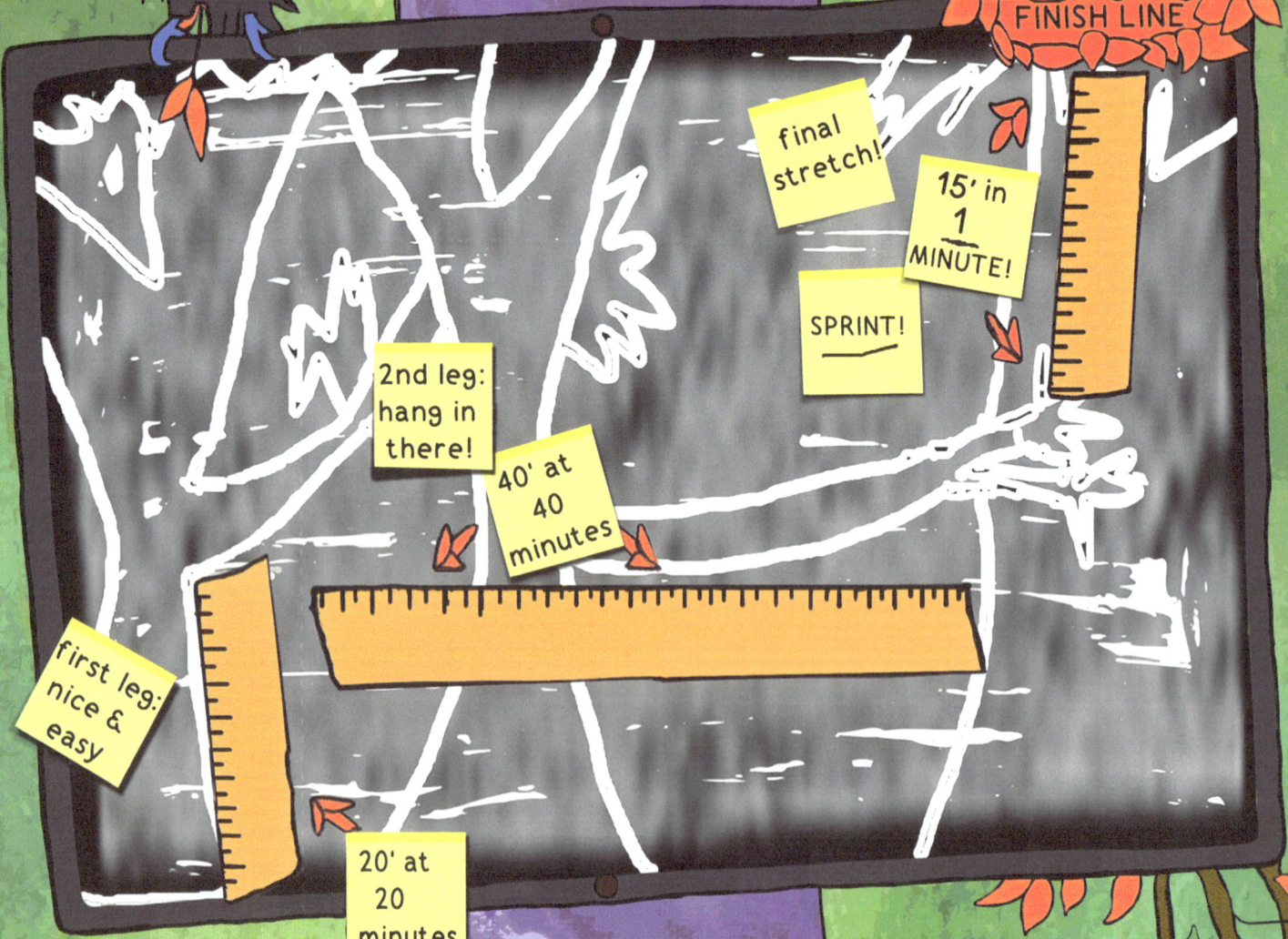

If ever in a race, he thought,
I'd be sure to win it.
I've timed my sprints at speeds
of up to fifteen feet per minute!

He challenged all the other sloths,
but none would take his bait.
They'd just look at him in
puzzlement, then say ...

"I'd rather wait."

Dude,
I'd rather wait.

DON'T HURRY,
BE SLOTHY

THEO
1st Place

So Theodore trained every day
   and worked on climbing trees,
while other sloths would hang
   around the limbs with lazy ease.

Theo cast hopeful looks
   as he madly dashed around,
But the other sloths just stared at him,
   then simply said, "Slow down!"

3
toes
rule

"Slow down?" Theo cried aloud.
"Whatever do you mean?
I've got the speed; I've got the drive;
I've got the golden dream!"

If it wasn't such an effort,
    the sloths might laugh in disbelief.
But that was too much trouble
    so instead ... they'd chew a leaf.

SLOW DOWN?

(Slow) Poke Salad*

Leaves (assorted)
Berries
(the tasty kind)
2 snails with shells
(adds crunch!)
Garnish with beetle

*lizard-free version

toes rule

Theo spied an inchworm,
   one day while he was training.
And after several minutes,
   it was CLEAR that he was gaining.

"I'll catch that worm! I know I can!
   I'll beat him to the top.
I've covered nearly FORTY FEET.
   Oh, no, I will not stop!"

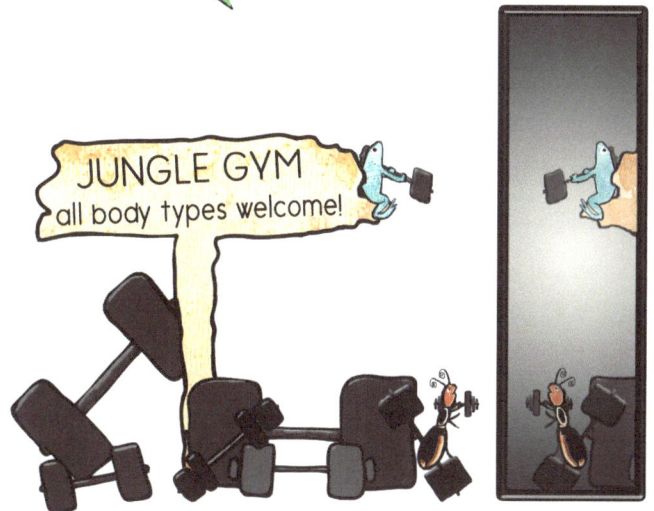

JUNGLE GYM
all body types welcome!

TREE LIFT

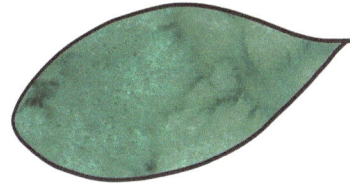

He reached the boughs
　　VICTORIOUS,
the champion of that tree.
　　His smile spread wide;
his eyes gleamed bright;
　　his heart filled up with glee.

Impatiently, he waited
　　for the inchworm to arrive.
The WINNER
　　of his first big race,
he finally felt alive.

"That was great!" he told the worm.
"I barely beat your pace!"

"What do you mean?"
replied the worm.
"Were we in a race?"

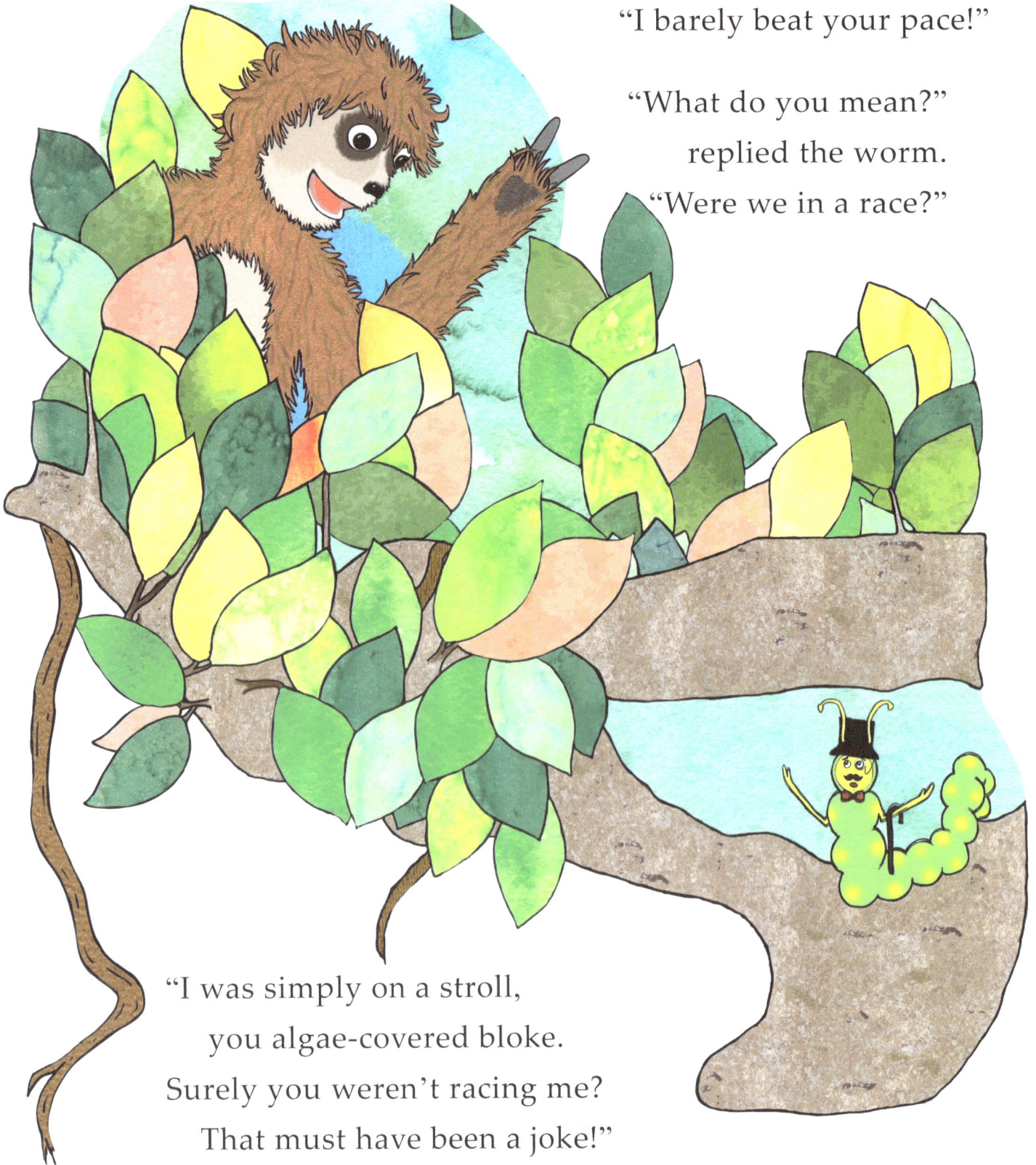

"I was simply on a stroll,
you algae-covered bloke.
Surely you weren't racing me?
That must have been a joke!"

Theo tried to laugh it off,
attempting to save face.

But deep inside,
our hero felt ashamed,
hurt, disgraced.

A smaller sloth was hanging near,
and said, "I know your pain.
The thankless hours, the sweat and tears,
the effort spent to train."

"For I, like you, have dreamed
of winning races filled with glory.
I, like you, have shared a place
in that all-too-tragic story."

NOTES:
Two-Toes
versus
Three-Toes

"I've challenged snails and slugs
and worms to name a few,
but Second Place has been my lot
in every race I knew."

"How can I lose, when I have DREAMED
to race around and hurry?"
Theodore groaned and moaned,
then snapped a branch in fury.

"I understand that bitterness,"
the smaller sloth replied.
"But one thing I have noticed:
you are MUCH faster than I!"

"Indeed, I do believe,"
Theo's new friend ventured on,
"the fact your toes are two,
not three, might help you speed along."

"And while I watched breathlessly
your record breaking pace,
I saw a few adjustments
that might help you WIN a race."

NOTES:
Two-Toes
versus
Three-Toes

Field notes:
1-10 scale

TREE LIFT

TREE LIFT

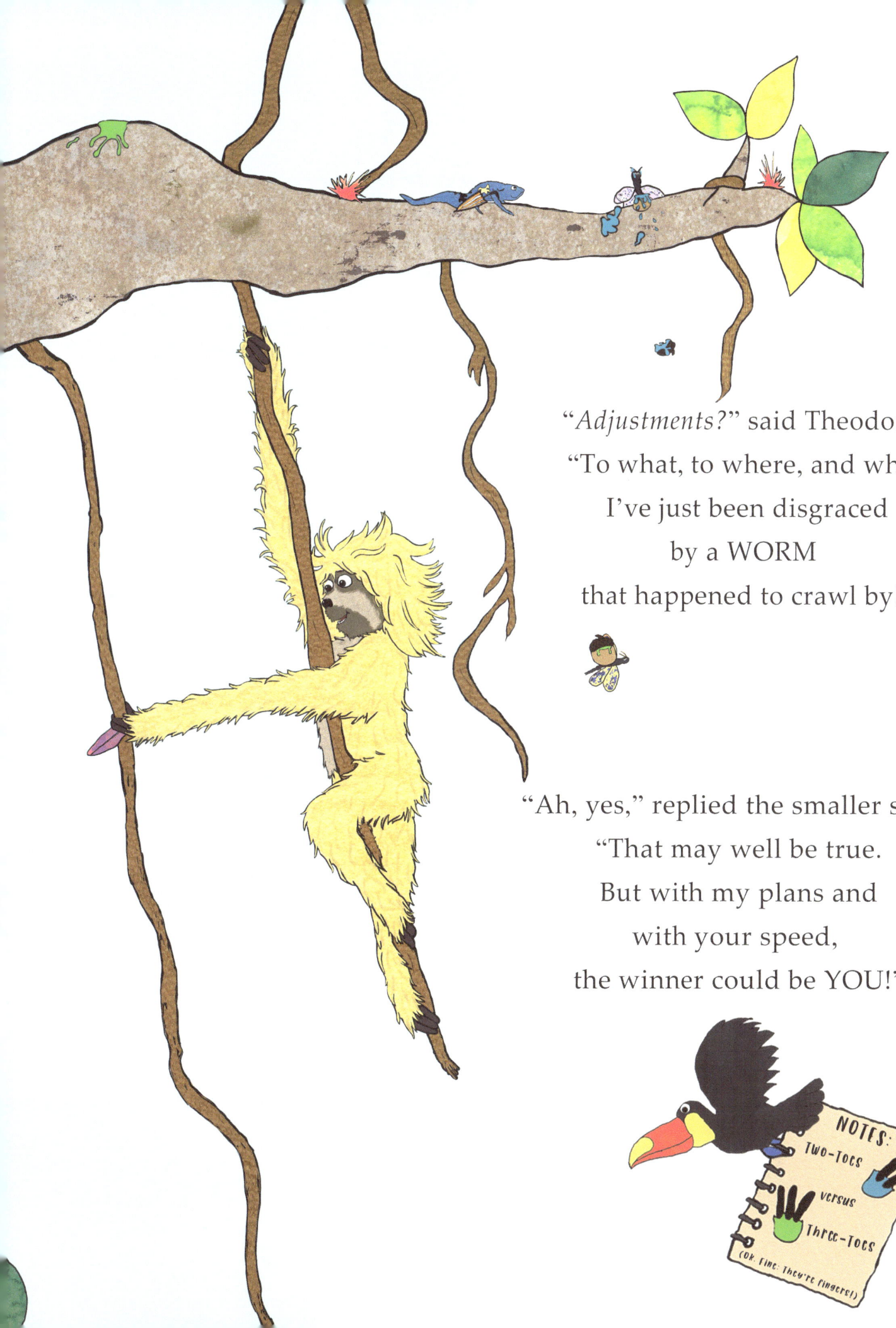

"*Adjustments?*" said Theodore.
"To what, to where, and why?
I've just been disgraced
by a WORM
that happened to crawl by!"

"Ah, yes," replied the smaller sloth.
"That may well be true.
But with my plans and
with your speed,
the winner could be YOU!"

NOTES:
Two-Toes
versus
Three-Toes
(OK, FINE: They're fingers!)

"How's that?" demanded Theodore.
"What is your magic cure?"

"Well, for starters, you'd be faster
without ALGAE in your fur."

"And furthermore," said his friend,
"you could try some squats.
To gain that extra burst of speed and give it

ALL

YOU'VE

GOT!"

"You're right! I still have HOPE!"
cried our hero in defiance.
"We all do!" said the smaller sloth.
"It's a matter of pure science."

"With systematic training,
we can learn to work and wean
Our slothful ways into those of a
FEARLESS RACE MACHINE!"

Then Theodore and his new friend began what now is known,
as the *Slothing Club For Those Who Need To Speed*, and it has grown,
From TWO members into FIVE!

And more are showing interest,

As Theo and the Slothing Club
train through sun

and tempest.

So if you're in the rainforest
and get lucky while you're there,
AND IF
you spy an athlete
without algae in their hair,

AND IF

they have a look
of pure determination
on their face ...

RAINFOREST
TOURS

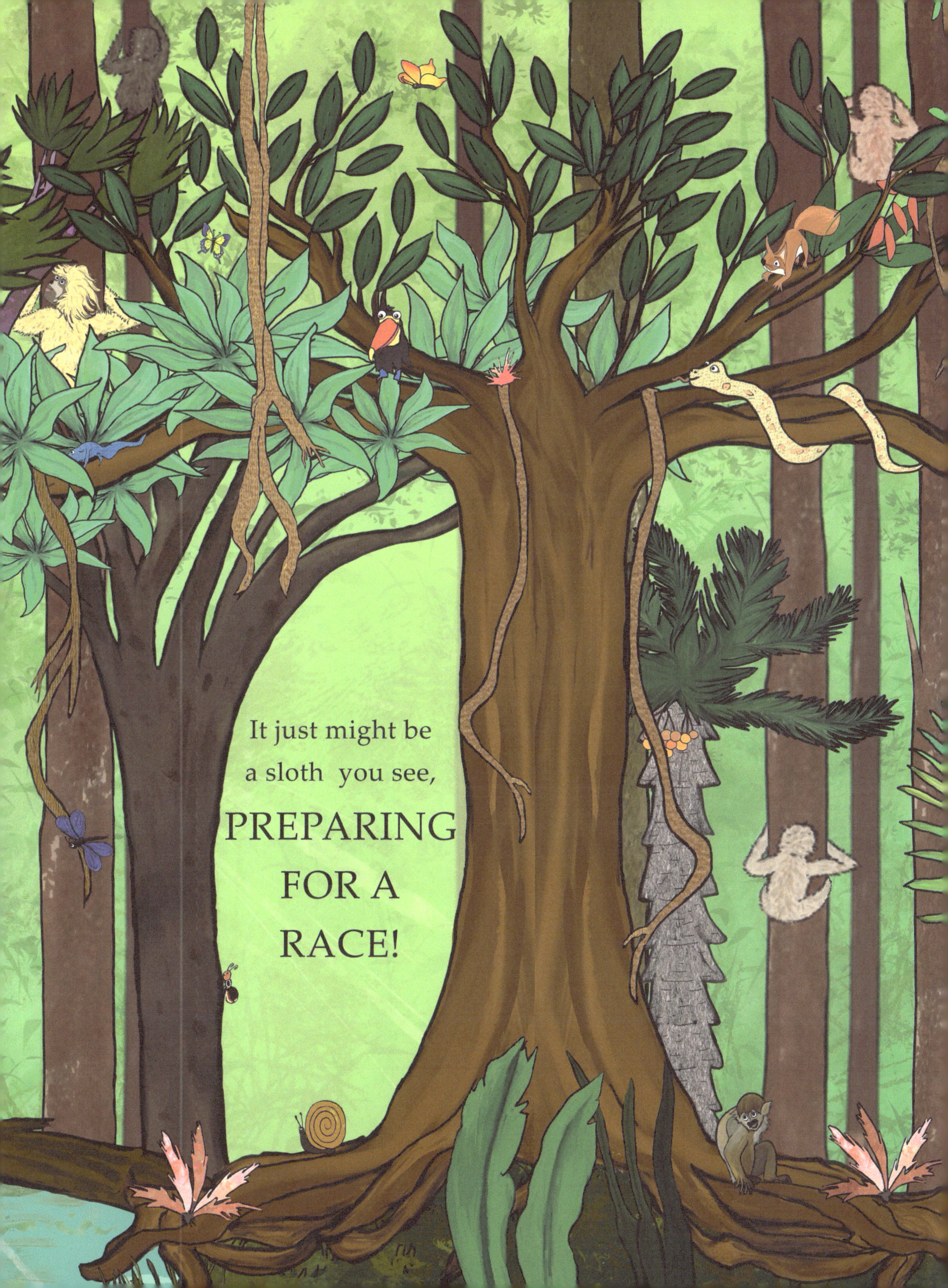

It just might be
a sloth you see,
PREPARING
FOR A
RACE!

Dr. Sam's Slothy Facts

🐌 There are six species of sloths, divided into two groups: Two-Toed and Three-Toed. Both groups have three toes on their back feet, but either two or three toes on their front feet.

🌵 These claw-like "toes" are actually extensions of their bones that stick out through the skin!

🐌 Two-toed sloths (like Theo) tend to be a bit bigger, and slightly less slow than three-toed sloths.

🌵 Who knew? Sloths are great swimmers!

🐌 Sloths climb down to the ground about once a week to go to the bathroom, and they always go in the same place.

🌵 Sloths are slowest on the ground. In the trees, they can sprint up to 15 feet per minute (but only in occasional, short bursts).

🐌 Sloths are so slow that they have algae growing in their fur. The main species of algae is special to sloth fur and not found anywhere else in the world. It is passed from mother sloths to their babies and helps provide camouflage.

🌵 Sloths usually hang out in a state called "Active Rest." This looks so much like sleep that we used to think they slept up to 20 hours each day. We now know that sloths in the wild sleep 8 to 10 hours each day. (Theo sleeps more since he's a growing athlete in training!)

Glossary of Super Words

Algae: Living things similar to plants that use sunlight for energy, but unlike plants, algae do not have roots, stems or leaves.

Apt: Likely or inclined to do or behave in a certain way. (As in, Dr. Sam is apt to enjoy ice cream!)

Bait: To tempt or try to lure someone or something.

Bloke: A casual (mainly British) word for a man or a male.

Contemplate: To think about something or to pay an idea special attention.

Defiance: To challenge authority; to do or say something that is different and often considered disobedient.

Ease: To move or act without difficulty or hurry.

Pace: How fast or slow someone/something is moving.

Puzzlement: To be puzzled or confused.

Slothful: To be lazy.

Systematic: To act in a steady and organized way.

Tempest: A storm.

Ventured: To go ahead or move forward with something even if there is risk or uncertainty.

Wean: To train or adjust someone or something to stop doing a certain behavior. (Example: We weaned our puppy from peeing on the carpet.)

A Game of Kingdom to Class

The Animal Kingdom is on full display at
the end of Theodore's story. Can you find each animal and put
them in the right Animal Classification? Follow the examples below!

Vertebrates:
(animals with a spine)

Amphibian

Bird

Fish

Mammal

Reptile

Ants
Bat
Beetles
Butterflies
Cayman
Dragonflies
Frog
Inchworm
Lizards
Monkey
Parrot
Piranhas
Sloths
Snail
Snake
Spider
Squirrel
Toucan
Turtle

Invertebrates:
(animals with no spine)

Arachnid

Gastropod

Insect

And how many animals can you count in total?

About the Authors

Dr. Sam practiced Veterinary Medicine for a number of years (he once was asked to treat someone's "kitty" that turned out to be a lion!) before deciding that he wanted to help people, too. So he went to medical school and now practices Family Medicine. He has worked in all kinds of places, including the USA, Germany, the Kingdom of Tonga, Samoa, China, Indonesia and Italy. In his free time, he writes jingles and funny stories with his wife, J.L. McCreedy.

J.L. McCreedy first discovered her love for writing (and developed an incurable condition of wanderlust) while growing up in Southeast Asia as a third-culture kid. She holds a Bachelor of Arts in English and a law degree, freelances as a writer and consultant for charitable organizations and, whenever possible, drags her splendid husband on ill-planned adventures.

Other books by J.L. McCreedy:

Liberty Frye and the Witches of Hessen
Liberty Frye and the Sails of Fate
Liberty Frye and the Emperor's Tomb
The Orphan of Torundi

Milton Keynes UK
Ingram Content Group UK Ltd.
UKHW051135261024
450169UK00008B/114